Earth's Many Landforms

I0811173

J. P. Haskell

INFOMAX COMMON CORE READERS

Rosen Classroom™

New York

Published in 2013 by The Rosen Publishing Group, Inc.
29 East 21st Street, New York, NY 10010

Book Design: Katelyn Londino

Photo Credits: Cover Caleb Foster/Shutterstock.com; p. 4 (mountain) Photodisc/Thinkstock.com; p. 4 (plains) Ablestock.com/Thinkstock.com; p. 4 (volcano) Zoonar/Thinkstock.com; pp. 4 (canyon), 11, 18 iStockphoto/Thinkstock.com; p. 5 Lee Prince/Shutterstock.com; p. 6 Pichugin Dmitry/Shutterstock.com; p. 7 skyearth/Shutterstock.com; p. 8 B.G. Smith/Shutterstock.com; p. 9 Top Photo Group/Thinkstock.com; p. 10 (canyon) Natalia Bratslavsky/Shutterstock.com; p. 10 (underwater canyon) Werner Van Steen/Stone/Getty Images; p. 12 meunierd/Shutterstock.com; p. 13 Tupungato/Shutterstock.com; p. 14 Darlene Cutshall/Shutterstock.com; p. 15 Design Pics/Thinkstock.com; p. 16 Joel Sartore/National Geographic/Getty Images; p. 17 Hemera/Thinkstock.com; p. 19 Tom Pfeiffer/VolcanoDiscovery/Photographer's Choice/Getty Images; p. 20 Jochem D Wijnands/The Image Bank/Getty Images; p. 21 MarekGahura/Shutterstock.com.

ISBN: 978-1-4488-9052-1
6-pack ISBN: 978-1-4488-9053-8

Manufactured in the United States of America

CPSIA Compliance Information: Batch #WS12RC: For further information contact Rosen Publishing, New York, New York at 1-800-237-9932.

Word Count: 423

Content

What Is a Landform? 4

Mountains 6

Valleys and Canyons 9

Moving Ice! 12

Flat Landforms 14

Volcanoes 18

An Adventure! 21

A Look at Landforms 22

Glossary 23

Index 24

What Is a Landform?

Earth's **surface** is always changing. It's covered with many different kinds of land. These are called landforms.

Some landforms are made when pieces of Earth's crust move. The crust is the top part of Earth. It's made of pieces that are always moving very slowly.

Mountains

Mountains are made when pieces of crust push against each other. A mountain is a very high piece of land.

A mountain rises up much higher than the land around it. The highest part of a mountain is called its peak. Some peaks are so high they have snow on them all the time!

A group of mountains is called a range. There are mountain ranges all over the world. A **famous** range in the United States is the Rocky Mountains.

Valleys and Canyons

A valley is a landform that you can see between mountains. The land in a valley is low. Rivers run through valleys.

A canyon is a deep valley between two **cliffs**. Rivers run through canyons. There are canyons on land and also under the sea!

The Grand Canyon is a famous canyon in the United States. It's in Arizona. It's very deep! You can see the Colorado River running through it.

Moving Ice!

Another kind of landform is a glacier. Glaciers are huge pieces of ice. These icy landforms move very slowly.

A moving glacier can cut into Earth's surface.

This forms a special kind of valley.

Flat Landforms

Some landforms are very flat. A plateau (pla-TOH) is a high piece of land that's like a mountain. Its top is much flatter than a mountain's pointed peak.

Plains are flat landforms, too. They're different from plateaus because they're low pieces of land. Plains are huge pieces of land with few trees.

There are plains all over the world. The Great Plains are in the United States. They're covered in grasses. Many animals live on the Great Plains.

The land on the Great Plains is good for farming. Wheat grows on these plains. People use this wheat to make bread.

Volcanoes

A volcano is another kind of landform. It's shaped like a cone and has a hole at the top. Volcanoes can be very tall.

Melted rock sometimes comes out of volcanoes. It comes from beneath Earth's crust. The melted rock is very hot! It forms new land when it cools.

Some volcanoes are under the sea. They make islands.

An island is a piece of land with water all around it.

An Adventure!

It's fun to look for different landforms. Looking for them is an **adventure**! What landforms can you see where you live?

A Look at Landforms

Glossary

adventure (uhd-VEHN-chur) An exciting trip or event.

cliff (KLIHF) A high, steep piece of rock.

famous (FAY-muhs) Very well-known.

melted (MEHL-tuhd) Made soft and flowing because of heat.

surface (SUHR-fuhs) The top part that can be seen.

Index

canyon(s), 10, 11, 22
cliffs, 10
Colorado River, 11
crust, 5, 6, 19
glacier(s), 12, 13, 22
Grand Canyon, 11
Great Plains, 16, 17
island(s), 20, 22
mountain(s), 6, 7, 8, 9, 14, 22
peak(s), 7, 14
plains, 15, 16, 17, 22
plateau(s), 14, 15, 22
range(s), 8
rivers, 9, 10
Rocky Mountains, 8
surface, 4, 13
valley(s), 9, 10, 13, 22
volcano(es), 18, 19, 20, 22